STORIES OF
COWBOYS

Russell Punter

Illustrated by Fabiano Fiorin

Reading Consultant: Alison Kelly
Roehampton University

Contents

Cowboy words

In this book, you'll find lots of special words used by cowboys. This list tells you what they mean.

bronco - a wild horse

calf - a young cow

cattle - lots of cows

corral - a big pen where cattle are kept

critter - a creature   **hogwash** - nonsense

prairie - a big, grassy area of land

lasso - a long rope with a loop at one end

pa - dad

ranch - a big farm for cattle

rodeo - a contest for cowboys

roundup - when cattle are gathered together by cowboys

rustler - someone who steals cattle

sheriff - a policeman

spur - a pointed piece of metal, often shaped like a star, on the back of a cowboy's boot

stagecoach - a small carriage pulled by horses

steer - a kind of bull

varmint - a bad person

3

Chapter 1

The rotten rustler

It was spring at the Silver Spur cattle ranch. Johnny Spur was helping with the roundup.

Johnny and his pa rode to the green fields. They rounded up the cattle...

led them down the hillside...

and into a corral.

There were eight calves.
Johnny's pa branded each one
with a little picture of a spur.

"Now folks will know they
belong to us," said
Johnny's pa.

The next morning, Johnny
went to feed the cattle. He soon
saw something was wrong.

...five, six,
seven...

"Quick, Pa!" yelled Johnny.
"Clementine is missing."

"Where the heck is she?" asked Mr. Spur.

A line of fresh hoof prints led out of the corral. Johnny and his pa followed the trail...

8

across the prairie...

to Hank Horseshoe's ranch.

"Did you steal my calf, Hank?" shouted Johnny's pa.

"Who, me?" said Hank. "I ain't no rustler."

"There's Clementine," cried Johnny, rushing up to a calf.

"She's mine," shouted Hank, pointing to his mark.

That's the Horseshoe Ranch symbol.

"Now get off my land!" roared Hank. "Or I'll set my dogs on you."

Johnny was sure Hank was a thief. That night, he hid by the corral and waited.

It wasn't long before Hank tiptoed up and took a calf. Johnny followed the sneaky rustler back to his ranch.

Hank pulled the calf into a barn. Johnny could clearly see the Spur mark on the calf.

Moments later, Hank and the calf came out. But now the calf had the Horseshoe mark.

Johnny crept into the barn.
He noticed some cans of paint
on top of a barrel.

Hank had fooled them! Now
Johnny had to prove it.

The next day, Johnny visited Hank's ranch. He took his pa and their friend, Chief Running Water.

"What do you critters want now?" yelled Hank.

"We've come for our cattle," said Johnny firmly.

"Well they ain't here," growled Hank. "So clear out."

"Not until the chief has done his rain dance," smiled Johnny.

Chief Running Water began to dance. It was a special dance to ask the sky spirits for rain.

"Ha!" snapped Hank. "I don't believe that hogwash."

There was an angry rumble of thunder, and rain pelted down.

Thank you, Chief.

The calves in Hank's corral were soaked. The rainwater washed away Hank's mark...

and showed the Spurs' symbol.

"Hank tricked us," explained Johnny. "He painted his mark over ours."

The stolen calves were soon back where they belonged. And the local sheriff put Hank where he belonged too – behind bars.

17

Chapter 2

Rodeo runaway

Pat Star was taking part in
the Cactus Valley Rodeo.
Cowboys had to ride a bull...

Go Pat!

then throw a rope
around a calf...

Pat and Tex Trapper were
the best after three events. The
final round was bronco riding.

The cowboys had to ride a wild horse for eight seconds. It wasn't easy.

Old Ben Creakwood only stayed on for two seconds.

Joe Lariat hung
on for five.

Wah!

But Tex
managed six.

Pat was the last to go.
"I gotta make sure Pat
doesn't beat me," thought Tex.

No one was looking, so Tex took an oil lamp...

and poured slippery oil on the bronco's reins.

"Let's see how long Pat lasts now," thought Tex.

Pat climbed into the bronco's saddle. The gate opened and the horse shot out.

Yee ha!

Poor Pat never stood a chance. The bronco bucked...

the reins slipped out of Pat's hand...

he went flying
through the air...

and hit the ground
with a thud.

The judges helped Pat to his feet. "I think my ankle is twisted," he sighed.

Ha ha!

BANG!

"Who's the best cowboy now?" boasted Tex. With a whoop of delight, he fired his gun in the air.

26

The sudden noise startled
Ned the pony. He was pulling a
wagonful of schoolchildren.

The terrified Ned galloped
out of the show ground and
into the desert.

"Somebody save them!" wailed the school teacher.

"Don't look at me," Tex muttered quietly.

Pat started limping to his horse, his ankle throbbing.

"Don't worry, ma'am," he cried. "I'll bring 'em back."

Pat raced out into the dusty desert. He rode as fast as he could until he saw the wagon.

Pat gasped in shock. The wagon was heading to the edge of a deep valley.

There was only one thing
to do. Pat rode alongside the
wagon and jumped onto the
runaway horse.

There were just seconds to spare. Pat tugged hard on Ned's reins. "Woooah, there!" he yelled.

"We're saved," cried the children. "What a hero!"

The rodeo judges agreed – and made Pat Star the King of the Rodeo.

Chapter 3

Wanted!

Chuck Parker wanted to be a cowboy on a ranch. Every day, he worked with his lasso.

His pa, the sheriff, wouldn't let Chuck lasso cows. So Chuck had to make do with chairs...

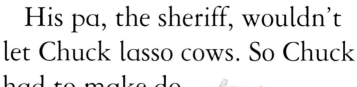

barrels...

fences...

and even Dusty, his dog.

Yelp!

Sheriff Parker didn't want his son to catch cows. He wanted him to catch crooks.

"Stop wasting your time with that rope," he moaned one day. "Take a look at this."

35

Sheriff Parker pinned a poster to the jailhouse wall.

WANTED!

DEAD OR ALIVE

BIG BAD BART

cattle rustler, bank robber and all-round sneaky critter

REWARD $500

"Keep a lookout for this varmint," warned Chuck's pa. "He's wanted all over Texas."

Chuck didn't think Bad Bart would ever visit their sleepy town. But he was wrong.

The very next day, a stagecoach pulled into town. The driver ran into the jailhouse and grabbed Chuck's pa.

"I've just been robbed,
Sheriff," panted the driver.
"He got away with six bags
of gold coins."

"What did the robber look
like?" asked Sheriff Parker.
The driver turned to the
poster. "That's him."

Chuck gasped. Bad Bart was on the loose nearby.

"He headed for Snake Creek," said the driver.

"I'll get your gold back," said Chuck's pa. He climbed onto his horse and rode off.

Chuck waited for his pa to return. He waited
all morning...

all afternoon...

and all night.

The next day, Chuck was too worried to wait any longer. He rode to Snake Creek as fast as he could.

I just hope Pa is okay.

Snake Creek was a spooky, lonely place. Chuck looked behind every rock and cactus. There was no sign of his pa.

Chuck had almost given up when he smelled smoke.

The smell led him to a small campfire. His pa sat nearby, all tied up. Chuck ran to him.

Keep back, son!

"What have we here?" growled a scary voice. Chuck turned to see Bad Bart towering over him.

"Okay Bart," said Chuck nervously. "Let my pa go and hand back the gold."

Bart roared with laughter.

Ha haa!

"Or what?" He chuckled. "Your pa couldn't stop me and neither will you."

"Time for me to leave camp,"
Bart shouted, shoving bulging
bags of gold into his saddle bag.

Bart rode off. Chuck had to
work quickly. He untied his pa
and made a loop in the rope.

45

Chuck swung the lasso and threw it over Bart. With a sharp tug from Chuck, Bart came flying off his horse.

Bart ended up in jail. And Chuck decided that catching crooks was even more exciting than catching cows...

especially after his pa made him Deputy Sheriff.

Series editor:
Lesley Sims

First published in 2007 by Usborne Publishing Ltd., Usborne House,
83-85 Saffron Hill, London EC1N 8RT, England. www.usborne.com
Copyright © 2007 Usborne Publishing Ltd.

48